Armond and the First Christmas

Luke 2:8-20, FOR CHILDREN

Written by Mary Curtin
Illustrated by Fred Womack

ARCH Books

Copyright © 1979 Concordia Publishing
House, St. Louis, Missouri
MANUFACTURED IN THE UNITED
STATES OF AMERICA
All Rights Reserved
ISBN 0-570-06129-6

Armond and Floppy heard a tune
As they stood out upon the hill.
They could not tell from where it came,
But Armond said, "Find it I will!"

They searched the bushes and the glen.
They looked in caves and valleys deep.
Ol' Floppy even used his nose
To sniff around among the sheep.

"Hey, Tinkle, do you hear the tune?"
Armond called to the leader ram.
"Do you hear it, Tink, my friend?
It sounds quite clear from where I am."

The sheep lay down, as if at rest.
The tune was putting them to sleep.
But Armond, Floppy, Tinkle, too,
Stayed up. The vigil they must keep.

For in their land the wolves did roam
In packs, to find a tasty meal.
And mutton was their favorite dish.
Armond knew they were near, and real!

The tune went on. All else was still
When Armond looked up in the sky.
He saw a vision floating there!
On wings of gold they seemed to fly.

Then, all at once, Armond was sure
The tune came from the vision bright!
They sang, "Peace on the earth, my friends!
A Child is born for you tonight!"

Armond stood and watched the angels
Singing words so sharp and clear.
They told him where to find the Babe.
And then the angels disappeared.

Armond and Floppy woke the sheep.
The sheep followed where Armond led.
The rocks were sharp. The hills were steep.
Poor Floppy's paws got cut. They bled!

15

Armond and Tinkle sped along.
Sometimes they ran, sometimes they walked.
The briers scratched and scraped their skin;
But, even so, no word they talked.

Armond led them to a town
Called Bethlehem. The hour was late.
Armond and Floppy, and the sheep,
Crept softly past the city gate.

The houses all were closed and dark.
The people slept. The town was still.
The little shepherd finally stopped
Near a stable on the hill.

It almost seemed the tune went on.
A glow was over all the scene.
It almost seemed that all the stars
Were twinkling gold and blue and green.

Then from the stable door they saw
A tiny baby on the hay.
Mary and Joseph were bending near
To warm and love Him where He lay.

The Baby's face held such a smile
Armond and Floppy stared in awe.
And Tinkle, with the other sheep,
Bent low in praise of whom they saw.

"Hello, Armond," the mother said,
Her voice so gentle and so sweet.
"I see you've scratches on your arms;
and little Floppy's cut his feet."

"It's nothing, Ma'am," the shepherd said.
"The angel sent us, with her tune,
To see God's Son, the Holy Babe.
Our wounds our small. They'll heal up soon."

How brave you are, dear little friends,
To bear these hurts to greet God's Son!
He'll not forget a love like yours.
God bless you, each and everyone."

Then, as she said these words to them,
The cuts and scrapes they did not feel.
And somewhere, in the sleepy town,
A tiny bell began to peal.

Armond, Floppy, and Tinkle, too,
Rose from their knees and backed away.
They'd always remember the angel's tune.
They'd not forget this holy day.

DEAR PARENT:

At the end of the Luke account of the story of the shepherds on Christmas Eve we are told: "When they told Mary and Joseph and others what the angel had said about this Child, all who heard them were amazed. . . . When the shepherds returned to their work, they praised God for what they had heard and seen" (Luke 2:17-20, *The Holy Bible for Children,* © 1977 Concordia Publishing House). What the shepherds had seen and heard was so amazing and wondrous they could not contain their excitement.

And how could anything else be the case, for how could news like this be contained?

This is how it should be with all Christians. It is impossible to contain our excitement and awe at this event, or the Gospel message. And though we don't know who the "others" referred to in vs. 17 were, we do know all who heard the shepherds' story were amazed.

It is our hope that every Christian responds to the Christmas story and the Gospel by telling others.

THE EDITOR